NO. IT'S PIG'S

This book belongs to:

~~Trevor~~